D1458808

SPIKE'S
BEST NEST

For Joan

Designed by Paul Cooper Design
Printed and bound in Belgium by Proost
for the publishers Piccadilly Press Ltd.,
5 Castle Road, London NW1 8PR

ISBN: 1 85340 485 3 (hardback)
1 85340 466 7 (paperback)

A catalogue record of this book is available from the British Library

Tony Maddox lives in Droitwich, Worcestershire. Piccadilly Press publish his tremendously successful books, *Spike the Sparrow Who Couldn't Sing*, *Fergus the Farmyard Dog*, *Fergus's Upside-down Day* and *Fergus's Big Splash*.

FERGUS THE FARMYARD DOG
ISBN: 1 85340 174 9

FERGUS'S BIG SPLASH
ISBN: 1 85340 388 1

FERGUS'S UPSIDE-DOWN DAY
1 85340 284 2

SPIKE, THE SPARROW WHO COULDN'T SING!
1 85340 196 X

FERGUS THE FARMYARD DOG – Book and Tape Pack
ISBN: 1 85340 445 4

SPIKE'S
BEST NEST

Tony Maddox

Piccadilly Press • London

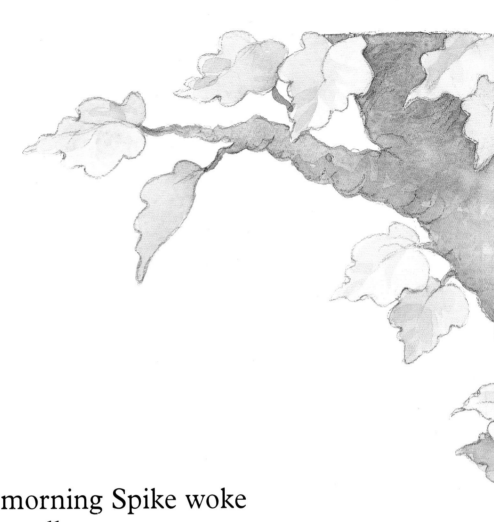

One morning Spike woke
feeling really grumpy.
He looked around and sighed.
"I'm bored with this old nest.
It's time I found somewhere
better to live."

He went to tell Wise Owl.
"I want to find a new place to live,"
he said, "so I won't feel so grumpy."

"Why not come and live with me?"
said Wise Owl. Spike was delighted.
"What a good idea!" he said.

That evening, Spike settled down to sleep in Wise Owl's nest. Just as he closed his eyes he heard, "Too-wit, Too-woo. Too-wit, Too-woo."

He looked out to see Wise Owl singing to the moon. "I'll never get any sleep here!" he groaned.

Feeling very tired, Spike set off early next morning to find somewhere new to live. At the farmyard, Mother Hen said, "Stay with me in the hen house."

But Spike wasn't very happy when
she left him to baby-sit her eggs!

"Come and live with us, Spike,"
said Freddie Fieldmouse
and he pointed to the ragged
scarecrow that stood in the big
cornfield.

But Freddie had
a very large family!

He went to the grassy hill where the rabbits played. "Come and share our burrow, Spike!" they said.

But when Spike peered into
the rabbit burrow, he saw it
was much too dark and gloomy.

The day was almost over when
he met the three green frogs.
"Come with us, Spike," they croaked.
"We know just the place for your new nest!"

They took him to their pond
and pointed to the lily pads.
"Choose any one you like," they said.

When night-time came,
Spike sat shivering on a
lily pad. It was cold and dark
and he felt very miserable.
Around him the frogs slept soundly.
He thought about his old nest
and how warm and cosy it had been.
He knew there was only one thing to do!

Later that night, Wise Owl flew by
Spike's old nest. He was surprised
to see someone asleep there.

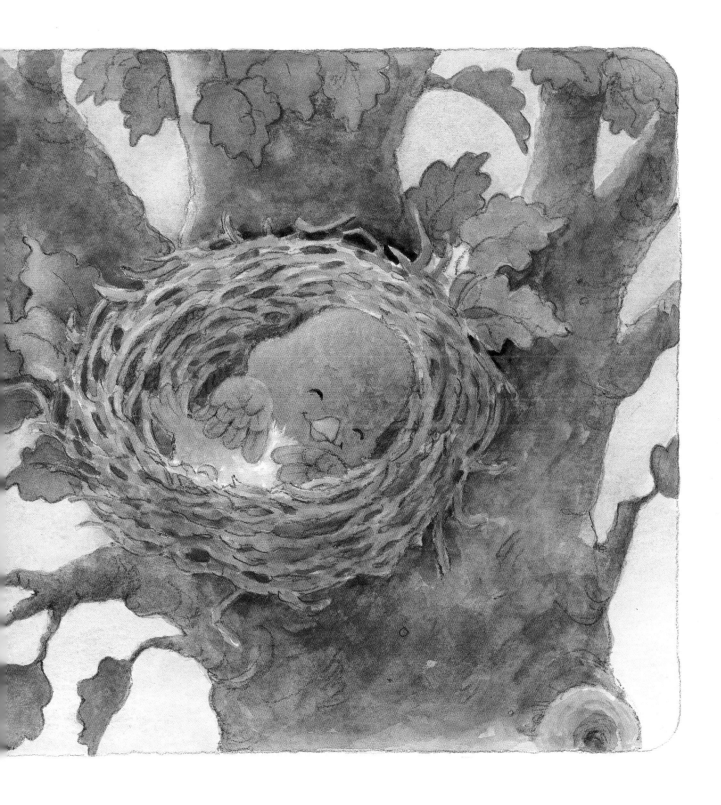

When he looked closer he saw
it was... Spike!

When Spike woke the next morning, he didn't feel grumpy any more. His nest was the best nest after all! And he sang the happiest song he knew.

The End